HOPSCOTCH
TWISTY TALES

Sleeping Beauty–
100 Years Later

by Laura North and Gary Northfield

W
FRANKLIN WATTS
LONDON•SYDNEY

This story is based on the traditional fairy tale,
Sleeping Beauty, but with a new twist.
You can read the original story in
Hopscotch Fairy Tales. Can you make
up your own twist for the story?

First published in 2010 by
Franklin Watts
338 Euston Road
London
NW1 3BH

Franklin Watts Australia
Level 17/207 Kent Street
Sydney, NSW 2000

Text © Laura North 2010
Illustrations © Gary Northfield 2010

The rights of Laura North to be identified as the author
and Gary Northfield as the illustrator of this Work have been asserted
in accordance with the Copyright, Designs and Patents Act, 1988.

A CIP catalogue record for this book is available
from the British Library.

ISBN 978 14451 0180 4 (hbk)
ISBN 978 14451 0186 6 (pbk)

Series Editor: Melanie Palmer
Series Advisor: Catherine Glavina
Series Designer: Peter Scoulding

Printed in China

Franklin Watts is a division of
Hachette Children's Books,
an Hachette UK company.
www.hachette.co.uk

For Paul – L.N.

A long time ago,
a King and Queen had
a beautiful baby daughter.

"Let's have a big party to celebrate," said the King. They invited everyone in the kingdom.

But they forgot to invite
one fairy.

She burst into the party in a rage. "I curse your daughter! She will cut her finger and fall asleep for a hundred years. Only a prince can wake her!"

"That will teach them to forget me!" she thought as she flew away.

The King and Queen were terrified. "No sharp things!" screamed the Queen, taking the knife and fork away.

"No playing outdoors!" said the King. The Princess wasn't allowed to do anything. She was miserable.

When the Princess reached her
18th birthday, the King and Queen
let her wander round the castle.

She found a room with an old spinning wheel.

The Princess was curious.
She tried making some thread
on the spinning wheel.

"Ouch!" she cried. She had pricked her finger on the needle. Suddenly, she fell into a deep sleep.

Everyone else fell asleep, too!
Years passed. Cobwebs
covered the castle.

15

One hundred years
later, a Prince wearing
sunglasses drove up to the castle.

He talked on a mobile phone.
He listened to music in earphones.
He wore jeans. A lot had changed
while the Princess had been asleep!

The Prince found the Princess. "What a sleeping beauty!" he thought. He went over to kiss her.

"Are you my Prince, my true love?"
asked the Princess, waking up.
"Just call me Harry," said the Prince.
"I'd like to take you on a date."

"A date?" said the Princess,
"I wonder what that is!"
Harry took her outside.
Everything looked so different!

"Is this your carriage? Where is the horse?" asked the Princess. "No need for one of those!" said Harry, starting the car engine.

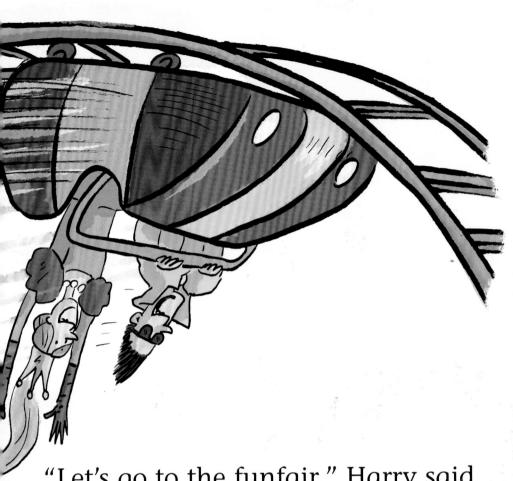

"Let's go to the funfair," Harry said.
The Princess whizzed around and
upside down on a rollercoaster.
"I've never had so much fun!"
she screamed.

Harry gave her a single red rose.

A thorn on the rose cut her finger.

"Oh no, what will happen to me now?" cried the Princess. "Will I fall asleep for another 100 years?"

"No, here's a plaster," said Harry
and he stuck it on her finger.

28

The Princess smiled. Life was so much better 100 years later!

Puzzle 1

Put these pictures in the correct order.
Which event do you think is most important?
Now try writing the story in your own words!

Puzzle 2

Choose the correct speech bubbles for each character. Can you think of any others? Turn over to find the answers.

Answers

Puzzle 1

The correct order is: 1e, 2d, 3f, 4a, 5c, 6b

Puzzle 2

The Princess: 1, 4

Harry: 2, 5

The bad fairy: 3, 6

Look out for more Hopscotch Twisty Tales and Fairy Tales: